WHAT TIME IS IT, MR. CROCODILE?

Judy Sierra

ILLUSTRATED BY Doug Cushman

Gulliver Books • Harcourt, Inc.   Orlando Austin New York San Diego Toronto London

Library of Congress Cataloging-in-Publication Data
Sierra, Judy.
What time is it, Mr. Crocodile?/Judy Sierra; illustrated by Doug Cushman.
p. cm.
"Gulliver Books."
Summary: Mr. Crocodile's plans to catch and eat some pesky monkeys do not work out and
he becomes friends with them instead.
[1. Crocodiles—Fiction. 2. Monkeys—Fiction. 3. Stories in rhyme.] I. Cushman, Doug, ill. II. Title.
PZ 8.3.S 577 Wh 2004
[E]—dc 21 2003004090
ISBN 0-15-216445-6

First edition
A C E G H F D B

Printed in Singapore

The illustrations in this book were done in acrylic on
gessoed Arches watercolor paper with collage additions.
The display type was set in Victoria Casual.
The text type was set in Neue Neuland and Victoria Casual.
Color separations by Colourscan Co. Pte. Ltd., Singapore
Printed and bound by Tien Wah Press, Singapore
This book was printed on totally chlorine-free Stora Enso Matte paper.
Production supervision by Sandra Grebenar and Ginger Boyer
Designed by Lydia D'moch

For irrepressible Lily
—J. S.

For Jackie, my true inspiration in Paris
—D. C.

Down by Bristlecone Bay, where the wifflefish play,
Mr. Crocodile, Esquire, is planning his day.

THINGS TO DO TOMORROW

9:00	wake up
10:00	eat breakfast
11:00	swim
12:00	go to town
1:00	visit the library
2:00	shop for food
3:00	bath and snack
4:00	catch those pesky monkeys
5:00	cook those pesky monkeys
6:00	eat those pesky monkeys
7:00	read a story
8:00	sing a lullaby to me

"Time to wiggle my toes. Time to put on my clothes. Time to brush every tooth till it sparkles and glows."

"Time to start off my day at the Stingray Café,
with a barnacle bagel and sea-slug soufflé."

"WHAT TIME IS IT, Mr. Crocodile?"

"Time to plunge in the bay,
time to splash, time to play.
Time to practice my
crocodile water ballet."

"WHAT TIME IS IT,
MR. CROCODILE?"

"Time to roll into town.
Time to twirl round and round.
Time to skate right side up,
or—YIKES!—upside down."

"WHAT TIME IS IT,
MR. CROCODILE?"

"Time to take a quick look
for a recipe book.
HURRY UP! HURRY UP!
I've got monkeys to cook."

Bananas
I
Have
Loved

A Monkey's Tail

Apes
in
the
Fog

King
Kong
My
Side

Cooking
AA-AW

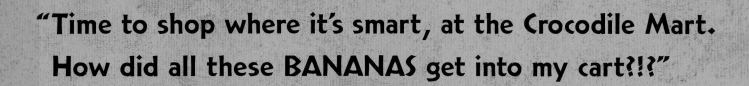

MR. CROCODILE?"

"Time to shop where it's smart, at the Crocodile Mart.
How did all these BANANAS get into my cart?!!?"

"Time to soak, time to dream,
time to plot, time to scheme.
Time to guzzle Croc-Cola
and seaweed ice cream."

"WHAT TIME IS IT, MR. CROCODILE?"

"Time to capture my meal as I sit at the wheel
of my marvelous monkey-collecting mobile."

"Time to cook? I'm too tired. I am SO-O-O uninspired—
'cause my plan to catch monkeys completely backfired."

"What TIME is it, Mr. Crocodile?"

"Time to say, 'I was rude, with a bad attitude,
and I'd much rather have you as friends than as food.'"

"What time is it, Mr. Crocodile?"

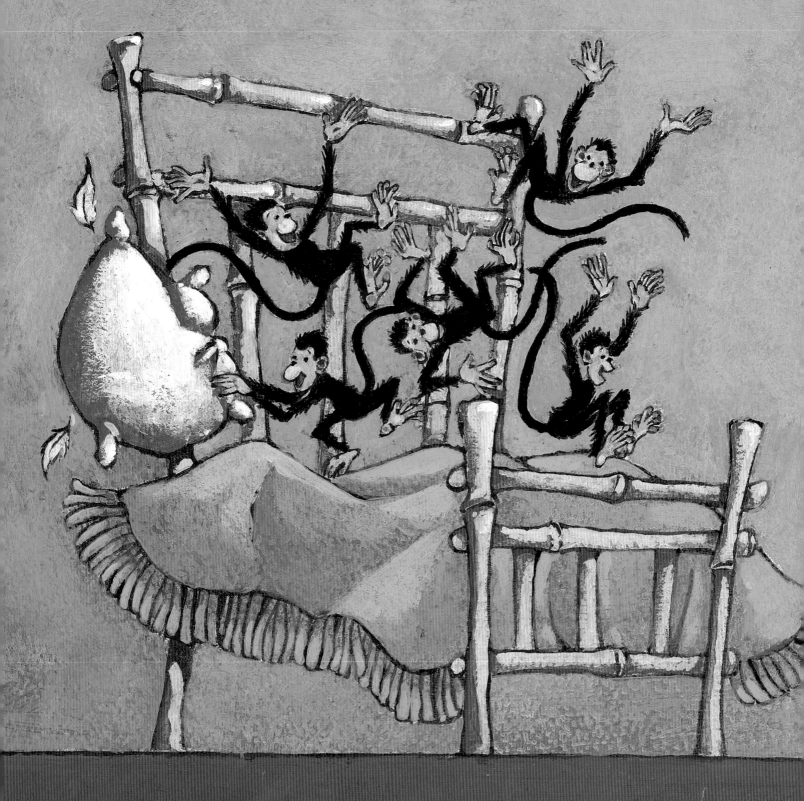

"Time to read about Fred, who bumped his poor head, and the five little monkeys that bounced on his bed."

"What time is it,
Mr. Crocodile?"

"Time to sing a sweet tune 'neath the crocodile moon.

Time to whisper, 'I hope you'll be coming back soon.'"

Down by Bristlecone Bay, where the wifflefish play,
Mr. Crocodile, Esquire, is planning his day.

THINGS TO DO TOMORROW

9:00   wake up

10:00   eat breakfast

11:00   teach monkeys to ∧ swim

12:00   go to town

1:00   visit the library — get good monkey stories!

2:00   shop for food — lots of bananas!

3:00   bath and snack

4:00   play ∧ catch ∧ with those nice ~~pesky~~ monkeys

5:00   cook for ∧ those nice ~~pesky~~ monkeys

6:00   eat with ∧ those nice ~~pesky~~ monkeys

7:00   read a story — no bouncing this time!

8:00   sing a lullaby to ∧ together ~~me~~.